John Smythe Hall

Speech Delivered at the Windsor Hall, Montreal

John Smythe Hall

Speech Delivered at the Windsor Hall, Montreal

ISBN/EAN: 9783337327927

Printed in Europe, USA, Canada, Australia, Japan

Cover: Foto ©Andreas Hilbeck / pixelio.de

More available books at **www.hansebooks.com**

SPEECH

Delivered at the WINDSOR HALL, Montreal, on 16th February, 1892, by

HON. JOHN S. HALL

Treasurer of the Province of Quebec,

On the Financial Affairs of the Province and Criticism of the Mercier Administration.

In making the remarks that I am going to make this evening with reference to the financial affairs of the Province of Quebec during the Mercier administration, and in offering my criticisms, which may seem to some harsh, but which I consider justifiable, there are four points to be well borne in mind :—

1st. The financial year runs from the 1st of July to the 30th June, and when I will hereafter speak of the years, it will be intended as referring to the year ending the 30th June.

2nd. In dealing with the figures, I will take the Public Accounts of the Province of Quebec as they have been printed under my predecessor, Hon. Mr. Shehyn.

I do not for a moment admit that the classification of the expenses into ordinary, extraordinary or special, as the case may be are correct, or that in many cases the entries properly represent what the transactions are.

In reading over speeches and discussions on our provincial finances, the wrangling has taken place as to whether items were chargeable as ordinary or extraordinary expenses or chargeable to capital. I would not attempt to settle the distinction with you to-night.

Mr. Shehyn introduced a new classification which he calls "Special" expenditure. This I do not think any one can accept, and it will be seen from the figures I will give you this evening that he puts "Repairs to Court Houses," "Iron Bridges," "Night Schools," "Books" and "Settlement of Claims," etc., all in this category of "Special Expenditures." It seems to me elementary that such expenses as these must come under ordinary expenditure. They are all recurrent or part of the policy of the Government.

However, we may as well, for the moment, close the discussion on the subject by the people consoling themselves with the fact that, whether it is ordinary, extraordinary, special or other expenditure, it has to be paid for out of revenue or earning power, and if you make loans for such purpose, repayment has to be made out of the earning power. It will be seen also that this so-called "Special Expenditure" has become a convenient heading to put payments under, to hide deficits in expenses, and that it has grown in amount annually and steadily.

3rd. The Public Accounts merely show a record of receipts and payments independent of whatever source they may be taken from, or paid out of, and, so much so, that temporary loans or trust funds, or deposits as guarantees from Railway Companies, are put down in the public accounts as a cash receipt, and merged into the ordinary cash, and when payments are made, such as payments of administration, the money may be taken out of the Loans, Trust Funds or Railway Deposits without it appearing in the general statement made by the Treasurer.

4th. The Hon. Mr. Mercier came into power on the 17th January 1887, in the middle of a financial year, and Hon. Mr. Shehyn, my predecessor, repudiates any responsibility with reference to the financial position or results or payments of the year 1887.

It will be my endeavour this evening to divide my remarks up in as clear and concise a manner as possible under the following heads :—

1st. The history and result of Mr. Shehyn's operations with the cash received and disbursed during the four years 1888, 1889, 1890 and 1891 and up to the 17th December 1891, for which he was responsible.

2. The present position of the Province as regards assets and liabilities.

3. The administration under Hon. Mr. Mercier's regime.

Before coming to these heads I may say, it may be that, in the course of my remarks, my language may seem to be a little strong, but I stand here to-night in the position of Provincial Treasurer, after having a comparatively short opportunity to investigate the affairs of the province. As a result I consider that the late administration was one of extravagance, carried into recklessness, and by reason of the extent of the latter, absolutely amounting to be corrupt.

I make these statements with a sole feeling of the duty imposed on me, and with a good deal of regret, because with the members of the late administration I was on the best of terms and received from them the utmost courtesy and consideration in any matters I had to do with them, either in respect to the affairs of my constituents or those of the city or province at large.

Now for the facts.

I do not propose to give you any figures that cannot be substantiated but I do feel that, while I have taken a certain amount of responsibility and am willing to assume it, yet, with the knowledge I have, I must and can relieve myself of a portion of that responsibility, by making the state of affairs known to you, and it will be for you, the people of the city of Montreal and this Province of Quebec to accept the consequences by your votes on the 8th March next, and decide whether the administration of the affairs of the province are to be continued by the party who have so maladministered them during the past four and a half years.

I.

THE HISTORY AND RESULT OF MR. SHEHYN'S CASH OPERATIONS.

I ask your patience to follow me closely in order that you may realize how dexterous my predecessor was, and with what subtlety and ability he hid from the public and the members of the Legislature what our true position was.

On the 12th April, 1887, the Hon. Mr. Shehyn made his first Budget speech in the Legislative Assembly. I listened to it with interest.

He commenced at the outset by assuring the House and the country he was going to deal with the finances "as a business man." He was held out to the country as such and we will soon see how far he has earned that reputation.

At the time, his speech gave, though at some length, a careful expose of the finances of the province, and of our assets and liabilities. He was quite severe on his predecessors, Hon. J. G. Robertson and prior administration, and used the strongest of language, making accusations, if not direct statements, of reckless, dishonest and wilful extravagance.

In that speech, Hon. Mr. Shehyn was full of promise and predictions of careful administration and honest and economical Government. I rather admired the speech, but, after he has had four years of trial, I find not only has every promise been violated but we have as a result, reckless and corrupt administration, our liabilities enormously increased, the burden of taxation raised, and yet our revenue totally inadequate to meet the present expenses.

The best proof of this is of itself evident when we consider that in the scarce five years of rule, Mr. Shehyn has made one permanent loan of $3,500,000, and a year ago obtained authority for a further loan of $10,000,000, of which $4,000,000 has been obtained and spent.

The net debt of this Province has been increased from $11,389,167.11 on the 17th January, 1887, to the sum of $24,423,683.62 on the 17th December, 1891. The annual ordinary expenses, according to Mr. Shehyn's own classification, have been increased from $3,032,771.45 (Public Accounts, 1886, p. 11) in 1886, to $4,095,520.45 in 1891, and the special expenditure, exclusive of railway subsidies, has run up from $177,000.00 in 1886, to $820,510.14 in 1891.

Mr. Robertson did not call this expenditure in 1886 "Special," but in his speech he attributed this expenditure, which was for the Parliament Buildings and Quebec Court House, to "Capital." All other expenses, excepting Railways, Repayment of Loans and Trust Funds, were charged to ordinary expenditure.

Mr. Shehyn in his speech declined to take any responsibility respecting the financial operations of 1886-87. He wanted to start with a clean slate, and in doing so he charged every expense and liability, possible and conceivable against his predecessors.

Owing to the extravagance, as he said, of his predecessors, the Ross-Taillon administration, the floating debt was large and he could not assume it, and he asked the House for a loan of $3,500,000.

If he got this he undertook anyway to satisfy all the obligations and deficits of the past, weather us through the perilous and orphan year of 1887 to which Mr. Shehyn would only be a step-mother, and for the financial year 1887-1888, for which he would be responsible, he would have a surplus of $19,693.20 (page 64 of his speech). He added, however, as the increase of from $2 to $5 had been made on the ground rents for timber limits on 7th April (five days before his speech), he should get a further revenue of $138,234.00 which would raise his surplus that year of 1888 to $157,927.00.

The House relied on his statements and figures and gave him what he wanted.

Let us now examine each year, what cash he received, and how he spent it.

It will be quite noticeable that Mr. Sheyhn was taking the cash received from trust funds, from temporary loans, and from guarantee deposits from railways, and employing these in the general cash. This had, as will be seen, but one result, that in a short time he had to have recourse to a loan to pay these back.

He was often attacked in the House for doing this, but his replies were so skilfully evasive as to delude most of the members of the Legislature, and his reputation as a business man led the people to have a false assurance in his statements.

1886-1887.

STATEMENT OF EXPENDITURES AND RECEIPTS, 1886–87.

Ordinary expenditure	$3,289,697 78	
do revenue	2,965,446 62	
Deficit of ordinary revenue to meet ordinary expenses........$	324,251 16	

SPECIAL EXPENDITURE.

Parliament Buildings	$ 184,298	00
Court House, Quebec	193,212	42
Court House Extension, Montreal	18,000	00
Railway Subsidies	736,896	70
Q., M., O. & O. Ry. construction acct	8,000	00
Hon. Thos. McGreevy, suspense acct	100,000	00
	$1,240,407	12

SPECIAL RECEIPTS.

Quebec Fire Loan	$ 120 00		
Municipal Loan Fund	5,380 00		
		$ 5,500	00

Excess of Special Expenditure over Special Receipts 1,234,907 12

Total excess of Expenditure over Revenue ....$ 1,559,158 28

PAID FROM THE FOLLOWING SOURCES :

Receipts on account of Advances and Trust Funds ....$	111,204 05		
Less payments on account of Advances and Trust Funds	18,510 75		
	$ 92,693 32		
Receipts from Temporary Loans ....$	600,000 00		
Re-payments of Temporary Loans	250,000 00		
	350,000 00		
Cash on hand; 30th June, 1886..$1,034,703 49			
Less outstanding warrants at that date, paid during the year	77,240 14		
	957,463 35		
		1,400,156 67	

Leaving an amount to be paid for which there were no funds on hand, amounting to .... $ 159,001 61

Represented by :

Outstanding warrants at 30th June, 1887...$	240,753 27		
Less cash on hand do ...	81,751 66		
		$ 159,001 61	

And at same date the Treasury was indebted for—

Temporary Loans	$1,100,000 00	
Trust Deposits	229,105 25	
		$ 1,329,105 25

The funded debt of the Province at this date was $18,854,353 34

As there appears to be a large amount of cash on hand on 30th June, 1886, it is only fair to explain this as follows :—

Cash on hand at 30th June, 1886, was.............................$	1,034,703 49
Less required to pay outstanding warrants at that date......	77,240 14
	$ 957,463 35

Of the $957,463 35 cash on hand 30th June, 1886, $622,464 00 was paid for railway subsidies before the 31st January, 1887, and $100,000 00 remained on Special Deposit in the Jacques Cartier Bank in connection with the claim against the Hon. Thomas McGreevy. This left the cash on hand at 30th June, 1886, $234,999 35 which was used for general purposes.

Mr. Shehyn then starts the year 1888 owing $1,488,106.86 for temporary loans and for monies received for trust deposits and for balance due on warrants outstanding in excess of cash on hand 30th June, 1887, but used up in the operations for the past year.

1887-1888.

Mr. Shehyn is entirely responsible for this year, and it is interesting to note the growth of the items under the head of "Special Expenditure," taken, as I consider in many cases, from ordinary expenditure simply to try and show a surplus in ordinary expenditure and receipts.

SYNOPSIS OF EXPENDITURE AND RECEIPTS, 1887-88.

ORDINARY EXPENDITURE, after deducting $55,844.93 of Crown Lands expenditure, transferred to Special Expenditure..........	$ 3,365,032 36	
Ordinary Revenue, including $721,213.95 being composed of $100,000 from the Province of Ontario ; $558,393, arrears direct taxes, and $62,820.95 from City of Montreal for arrears (part of $125,000 received, the balance included in Special Receipts).	3,738,228 39	
Surplus of ordinary revenue over ordinary expenses .... $	373,196 03	

SPECIAL EXPENDITURE—

Parliament Buildings....................... $	250,000	00
Court House, Quebec	210,000	00
Court House extension, Montreal..........	21,422	83
McGill Normal School	2,500	00
Arthabaska Court House and Gaol........	6,000	00
Heating Apparatuses, Court Houses and Gaols..	6,000	00
Court House and Registry office, Kamouraska..	6,000	00
Iron Bridges	25,000	00
Codification of the Laws	45,000	00
Explorations in Dorchester, etc..............	10,000	00
Crown Lands Department.—Expenditure to meet old engagements transferred from Ordinary Expenses....................	55,844	93
Railway Subsidies..............................	648,275	30
Q. M. O. & O. Ry. construction acct........	14,000	00

$ 1,300,043 06

SPECIAL RECEIPTS—

Quebec Fire Loan .... $	540	00	
Municipal Loan Fund	4,891	23	
Montreal contribution to Hull bridge (part of $125,000).....	25,444	00	
Montreal contribution to cost of land between Hochelaga and Dalhousie Square (part of $125,000)	36,735	05	
Q. M. O. & O. Ry., refunds, etc.	316	13	

$ 67,926 41

Excess of Special Expenditure over Special Receipts......... $ 1,232,116 65

Total excess of expenditure over revenue during year........ $ 858,920 62

Add excess of outstanding warrants at 30th
June, 1887, over Cash on hand at that
date, viz.:—Cash on hand at 30th June,
1887.. $ 81,751 66
Outstanding warrants at that date........... 240,753 27

159,001 61

$1,017,922 23

PAID FROM THE FOLLOWING SOURCES :—

Receipts on account of Advances and Trust Funds		$ 54,588 81	
Less payments on account of Advances and Trust Funds		51,667 83	
		$ 2,920 98	
Receipts from Temporary Loans	$ 400,000 00		
Receipts proceeds of Loan 1888	3,378,332 50		
	$3,788,332 50		
Re-payments, of temporary loans	1,500,000 00		
		2,278,332 50	
			$ 2,281,253 48

Balance of gross receipts over gross payments .... $ 1,263,331 25

During this year Mr. Shehyn effected the loan of $3,500,000.00, and at the end of the year this balance was represented by :—

Cash on hand at 30th June, 1888	$ 1,723,850 07
Less required to pay outstanding warrants	460,518 82
	$ 1,263,331 25

Being the amount remaining of the $3,378.332.50, proceeds of the loan of 1888 and other receipts, the temporary loans of $1,100,000.00 unpaid on 30th June, 1887, having been paid out of proceeds of said loan.

The Treasury Department was indebted for Trust Deposits at same date in the sum of....................................	229,026 23
The funded debt of the Province at this date was	22,354,353 34

Mr. Shehyn then, to start the year 1888-1889, had, through the advantage of the loan, $1,263,331.25 cash on hand, including $229,026.23 of Trust deposits, though, as we will see later, a considerable amount of the obligations for which the loan of $3,500,000.00 was contracted, still remained owing.

In his speech on the 15th February, 1889, (page 7) Hon Mr. Shehyn said, "We have to acknowledge, for 1888, a surplus of $373,000 in the ordinary receipts over the ordinary expenditure."

I think I will show that his surplus of $157,927 promised in his April speech of 1887 was gone, and the $373,000 is a myth. He received the following sums which he never anticipated or never calculated upon, and, in fact, they are not even hinted at in his speech of 1887 :—

From Ontario School Fund	$100,000 00
Arrears Commercial Corporation Tax	558,393 00
City of Montreal, settlement	62,820 95
	$721,213 95
Deduct supposed surplus	$373,000 00
Actual deficit	$348,213 95

Not including $135,000, at least, charged to special expenditure, which was really ordinary expenditure.

Mr. L. G. Desjardins criticized very fiercely and properly the prognostications and administration of Mr. Shehyn, and cited the above figures. Mr. Robertson and myself followed Mr. Desjardins, and by dint of hammering compelled Mr. Shehyn to reply and state the facts. He did so, and in his subsequent speech delivered on the 8th March, 1889, at page 21, referring to the year 1888, Mr. Shehyn said he admitted this, and said, "according to my estimates I counted upon a total of $3,020,522.80 of "ordinary receipts, not including $40,000 received from the common school "fund over and above the $60,000 upon which I counted, when I made my "estimates, nor the $557,665 and the $100,000 of increase in other services "which I had not included in the same forecast." He alluded of course to the forecasts in his speech of 1887.

CITY OF MONTREAL SETTLEMENT.

On 8th August, 1887, the Government had a claim against the city for unsettled accounts of previous years amounting to $245,637.46 for maintenance of insane, and of prisoners, for gaol guards, subscription to Hull bridge and for cost of lands expropriated for railway from Hochelaga to Dalhousie square. It was settled for $125,000; of this $62,320.95 was placed as above mentioned as an "ordinary" receipt, and the balance $62,179.05 as a "special" receipt.

Then for the year 1888-89 he estimated, (page 47, speech, 14th June, 1888), in ordinary expenses and receipts a surplus of $68,413.06. The following is a synopsis of that year's transactions, taking again Mr. Shehyn's own classification of expenditure :—

1888-1889.

SYNOPSIS OF EXPENDITURE AND RECEIPTS, 1888-89.

Ordinary Expenditure	$3,543,618 64	
" Revenue	3,625,115 20	
Surplus of Ordinary Revenue over Ordinary Expenses		$ 81,496 56

SPECIAL EXPENDITURE.

Parliament Buildings	$125,729 53
Court House, Quebec	42,733 59
Court House Extension, Montreal	50,000 00
Arthabaska Court House and Gaol	1,400 00
Heating Apparatuses Court Houses and Gaols	6,000 00
Court House and Registry Office, Kamouraska.	4,000 00
Bonaventure Court House and Gaol	4,000 00
Iron Bridges	50,000 00
Codification of the Laws	26,324 40
Explorations in Dorchester	10,000 00
Compensation for errors in Surveys, Rouville	10,500 00
Spencerwood, Stables, &c.	4,000 00
Purchase of Seed Grain	50,000 00
Arbitration between Quebec and Ontario...	1,673 72
Lockwood's Claim	10,000 00
Quebec Railway Bridge	1,277 16
Railway Subsidies	1,049,847 00
Q. M. O. & O. Railway Construction Acc't..	26,800 00
	$1,474,285 40

SPECIAL RECEIPTS.

Quebec Fire Loan	$ 360 00	
Municipal Loan Fund	85,538 60	
McGill Normal School Refund	2,454 00	
		$88,352 60
Excess of Special Expenditure over Special Receipts		1,385,932 80
Total excess of Expenditure over Revenue during year		1,304,436 24

PAID FROM THE FOLLOWING SOURCES:

Receipts on account of Advances and Trust Funds... $	54,427 42		
Railway Companies' Guarantee Deposits.....................	2,229,670 45		
		$2,284,097 87	
Less payments on account of Advances and Trust Funds. $	48,317 52		
Repayment Railway Guarantee Deposits.....................	57,915 23		
		106,232 75	
		$2,177,865 12	
Cash on hand at 30th June, 1888..............................	$1,723,850 07		
Less outstanding Warrants, 1888...............................	460,518 82		
		1,263,331 25	
			3,441,196 37

Balance of gross receipts over gross payments.................		2,136,760 13
Represented by:		
Cash on hand at 30th June, 1889..............	$2,210,019 79	
Less outstanding Warrants at 1889...........	73,259 66	
Leaving an available balance of.......................................		2,136,760.13

This was after having used up the balance of the loan of 1888, and the Treasury was indebted at the same date for:

Balance of railway guarantee deposits received during the year	2,171,755.22
Trust Deposits...	262,947.48
	2,434,702.70

The funded debt of the Province at this date was.............. $22,354,353.34

Mr. Shehyn now starts the year 1889-1890, owing in cash $297,942.57; that is the difference between the cash on hand and the amount of railway and trust deposits. The loan of $3,500,000.00 has been all spent, and many of the obligations for which it was contracted remaining, as will be seen, unpaid. See Statement L annexed.

In his speech on 21st February, 1890, (page 10), Mr. Shehyn congratulates himself on a surplus of $84,565.56. Here again he would have been sadly out of his reckoning, did he not include the sum of $118,097 proceeds of sales of timber limits, which fell into the cash for the year 1889.

Taking again his own figures and classification, the operations for 1889-90 were as follows :—

1889-1890.

SYNOPSIS OF EXPENDITURE AND RECEIPTS, 1889-90.

Ordinary expenditure	$3,881,672	95
" revenue	3,536,783	79

Deficit of ordinary revenue to meet ordinary expenses...... $344,889 16

SPECIAL EXPENDITURE :

Parliament Buildings	$162,760	00
Court House, Quebec	49,037	86
New vaults for Court Houses and Gaols	4,534	47
Kamouraska Court House and Registry Office	2,512	00
Iron Bridges	76,460	42
Codification of the Laws	86,675	00
Explorations in Dorchester	9,824	50
Spencerwood, Hot-house, cellar, &c	10,231	00
Quebec Railway Bridge	404	53
Night Schools	19,737	45
Bibliothèque du Code Civile	6,000	00
Dictionnaire Numérique de Boucherville	2,785	00
Heirs late John Langelier	5,000	00
Speaker's portraits	1,600	00
Repairs Brother Arnold's School	999	88
Library late Judge Polette	8,000	00
Heirs late Judge Loranger	2,182	40
New Map, Province of Quebec	10,200	00
Corporation City of St. Johns	3,500	00
Installation Houses of the Legislature	4,640	00
Printing, binding, etc., of the laws to correct omission in 1878	6,500	00
Settlement of the Jesuits' Estates	400,000	00
Railway Subsidies	827,417	97
Q. M. O. & O. R'y construction account	10,000	00
	$1,162,001	48

SPECIAL RECEIPTS :

Quebec Fire Loan...	$623 28	
Municipal Loan Fund............	3,200 00	
Jesuit Barracks property........	30,000 00	
		33,823 28

Excess of Special Expenditure over Special Receipts......... 1,128,178 20

Total excess of Expenditure over Revenue during year...... 1,473,067 36
Add payments on account of
Advances and Trust Funds... 14,163 98
Repayment R'y Guarantee De-
posits 255,069 24
                               269,233 22
Less receipts on account of Advances and
Trust Funds.. 18,313 43
                                     250,919 79

                                   1,723,987 15

PAID FROM THE FOLLOWING SOURCE :

Cash on hand at 30th June,
1889............................... 2,210,019 79
Less outstanding warrants, do 73,259 66
                                 2,136,760 13

BALANCE OF GROSS RECEIPTS OVER GROSS PAYMENTS........ 412,772 98

REPRESENTED BY

Cash on hand at 30th June, 1890............. $525,344 43
Less outstanding warrants, do. 112,571 45
                                 412,772 98

At the end of the year 1889–1890, the situation was getting critical, though carefully concealed by Mr. Shehyn, and these are the facts :

The cash available was... 412,772.98

Nothing remained of the proceeds of the loan of 1888.

The Treasury Department was indebted for Railway Guar-
antee Deposits... $1,916,685.98
Trust Deposits 261,361.27

                                 $2,178,047.25

The funded debt of the Province at this date was............ $22,354,353.34

Mr. Shehyn now starts the year 1890-91 owing, over and above the cash on hand, $1,765,274.27 for trust funds and Railway Guarantee deposits, which he has used up, and his loan of $3,500,000.00 is all gone? The climax had to come.

In the meantime, in June, 1890, the local elections took place. Everywhere we heard of the good administration of Mr. Shehyn and the splendid financial position of the Province. The era of deficits had gone.

Mr. Robertson, Mr. L. G. Desjardins and myself during the various sessions tried to warn the people and expose the facts. Mr. Shehyn was still heralded as a "business man," and most people took his word. The majority of the members of the Legislature still believed him, and the public relied on him. What was the result?

The new Legislature met in November, 1890, and Mr. Shehyn made his confession in his speech in the House on the 5th December, 1890. He admits his deficit in ordinary working expenses of $344,000.00 odd for that year, even according to his own classification. As to his special and ordinary expenditure, it was difficult for him to say where he was, every one was to blame but himself. He could not check, he said, the expenditure or control the service. It was the House was to blame for voting monies, subsidies, &c., yet he never once pointed out in any of his speeches where we were going, or that we were face to face with increased taxation and increased loans.

His speech is long in trying to extricate himself, but, to make a long story short, after hiding it from the people for years, he has to admit a floating debt of $6,762,033.86 on 30th June, 1890, (page 25 of his speech) that he has no means of paying off.

Notwithstanding this, after this date in June, reckless expenditure goes on, and on the 30th December, 1890, when the Legislature met, a bill was introduced authorising a further loan to the extent of $10,000,000.00 to provide for the floating debt on 30th June, 1890, consequent on Mr. Shehyn's administration, and to meet the obligations, the ordinary revenue was insufficient for, imposed under the Mercier administration.

The $10,000,000.00 loan was based on the floating debt of the Province as on 26th December, 1890, and that floating debt was described in the act as follows:

(54 Vic., Cap. 2.)

Outstanding warrants	$ 112,571	45
Temporary deposits	261,361	27
Railway guarantee deposits	1,916 685	98
Railway subsidies granted, but not yet earned	2,898,247	88
Debts Q. M. O. & O. Ry	122,364	00
Loss Exchange Bank deposit	27,000	00
Protestant settlement Jesuits' Estates	62,961	00
Estimated Special Expenditure 1890-91	912,183	00
	$ 6,313,374	58
Less cash on hand 1st July, 1890	525,344	43

Supplementary Special Expenditure 1890-91...................	115,488 71
Estimated Special Expenditure 1891-92.........................	588,555 00
Railway subsidies voted in session of Nov. & Dec., 1890.....	4,400,320 00

$10,862,353 86

If ever improvident, reckless and extravagant administration existed, taking into consideration his previous declarations, the above figures and statements show it.

I have digressed a little as a matter of history and date to show what took place after the 30th June, 1890.

1890-91.

Turning again to the cash operations and taking the year 1890-91, the following is the result. It will be amusing to see now the growth of items under the head of "Special Expenditure," and the absurdity of not including the majority of them in ordinary expenditure :—

SYNOPSIS OF EXPENDITURE & RECEIPTS, 1890-91.

Ordinary expenditure	$4,095,520 45
do revenue	3,457,144 32

Deficit of ordinary revenue to meet ordinary expenses....... $638,376 13

SPECIAL EXPENDITURE.

Parliament Buildings.............................. $	13,495 34
Court House, Quebec...............................	159,007 00
Montreal Court House extension...............	150,000 00
New vaults for Court Houses and Gaols.....	7,000 00
Heating apparatuses, Court Houses and Gaols	8,000 00
Sherbrooke Court House and Gaol............	8,000 00
Gaspe, do do	2,286 00
Quebec Gaol.................	8,890 00
Iberville Court House and Gaol...............	8,000 00
New Gaol, Montreal..............................	27,263 44
Iron Bridges......................................	100,000 00
Spencerwood, hot-house and cellar............	1,000 00
Quebec Railway Bridge..........................	1,750 00
Night Schools....................................	40,000 00
Stoning country roads............................	6,315 23

Colonization roads, explorations, &c..........	50,000 00	
McGill Normal School, Montreal..............	60,805 00	
Exhibition Society, to repair buildings, Montreal	25,000 00	
Exhibition Grounds, Montreal..................	28,721 90	
Toronto University, in aid of reconstruction	10,000 00	
For damages by wind storm in Beauharnois, Vaudreuil and Huntingdon..................	9,880 00	
Revised Statutes towards supplementary volume	6,009 84	
Arts and Manufactures Building, Quebec...	5,532 00	
Jacques Cartier Normal School, Montreal...	80,000 00	
General Index, Journals of Leg. Assembly	6,000 00	
Memoir Chevalier de Levis....................	3,150 00	
Expenses, illness and funeral Mgr. Labelle	2,942 30	
Commission re culture of beet-root, on acc't.	6.206 00	
Railway subsidies.................................	885,255 00	
Q. M. O. and O. Ry. construction account	70,364 27	
Special Expenditure (there being no Special Receipts)		1,775,874 41
Total excess of expenditure over revenue during year		2,414,250 54

PAID FROM THE FOLLOWING SOURCES:

Receipts on account of Advances and Trust Funds..	$ 15,149 02		
Railway Company guarantee deposit	278,520 00	293,669 02	
Less payments on account of advances and trust funds	57,177 42		
Repayment Railway Guarantee deposits	222,097 41		
		279,274 83	
		14,394 19	
Receipts from Temporary Loans		2,223,333 33	
Cash on hand at 30th June, 1890.......................	525,344 43		
Less outstanding warrants at 30th June, 1890.........	112,571 45		
		412,772,98	2,650,500 50
Balance of Gross Receipts over Gross Payments......			236,249 96

Represented by:

Cash on hand at 30th June, 1891	471,852 59	
Less outstanding warrants at 30th June, 1891	235,602 63	
		236,249 96

The available cash on this date was ....$ 236,249 96

And the Treasury Department was indebted for—

Temporary Loans	$ 2,223.333 33	
Railway Guarantee Deposits	1,973,108 57	
Trust Deposits	262,252 47	
	$ 4,458,694 37	

The funded debt of the Province at this date was.............. $22,354,353 34

The year 1891-92 was then started by the Province owing for temporary loans, trust funds and railway guarantee deposits, the enormous sum of $4,222,414.41 over and above the cash on hand received and put into general purposes and not a cent to pay this out of except the hopes of the new $10,000,000.00 loan and to say nothing of the enormous new obligations for new expenditure and new railway subsidies and items of floating debt.

1891 TO 17TH DECEMBER.

I now come to a difficult point in showing the cash operations up to 17th December, 1891, when the Mercier administration were dismissed, and in giving an estimate of what will be required and what will be the result on 30th June, 1892. The books, however, up to 17th December, 1891, show the following, bearing in mind that $4,000,000 or thereabouts of the $10,-000,000 loan has been received and exhausted:

SYNOPSIS OF EXPENDITURE AND RECEIPTS FROM THE 1st JULY TO THE 17th DECEMBER, 1891.

Ordinary expenditure	2,083,015 47	
Ordinary revenue	1,534,938 35	
Deficit of ordinary revenue to meet ordinary expenditure		548,077 12

2

SPECIAL EXPENDITURE:

Parliament Buildings..........................	7.788	93
Montreal Court House extension............	42,086	23
Heating apparatuses Court House & Gaol....	12,000	00
Bryson Court House and Gaol.................	6,321	10
New Gaol, Montreal...........................	144	00
Iron Bridges...................................	22,234	58
Spencerwood, Porter's Lodge.................	600	00
Night Schools.................................	23,044	36
Stoning Country Roads........................	31	95
Laval Normal School, new building...........	852	40
Edifice Nationale, Montreal..................	5,000	00
Kamouraska Court House Debentures.........	8,105	00
Commission re-Culture of Beet Root	4,909	85
Royal Commission re Baie des Chaleurs Ry	10,000	00
Railway Subsidies.............................	325,855	00
	468,973	40

SPECIAL RECEIPTS.

Municipal Loan Fund...................3,000 00			
Reimbursement Railway Subsidies			
Fund 3,847 10			
		6,847	10

Excess of Special expenditure over Special		
Receipts..	462,126	30
Total excess of expenditure over Revenue to		
17th December, 1891.....................	1,010,203	42

ADD PAYMENTS ON ACCOUNT OF :

Advances and Trust Funds.........	7,383 40		
Repayment Ry. guarantee...........			
Deposits 112,342 93			
		119,726	33
Less receipts on account of Trust Funds......	3,374 18		
		116,352	15
		1,126,555	57

PAID FROM THE FOLLOWING SOURCES :

Cash on hand 30th June, 1891	471,852	59
Less outstanding warrants at 30th June,		
1891, paid between 1st July and 17th		
December, 1891..........................	235,602	63
	236,249	96

Proceeds of Loan, 1892.............3,707,530 00
Repayment of Temporary loans..2,073,333 33   1,634,196 67   1,870,446 63

Balance of gross receipts over gross payments   743,891 06

   Represented by—

Cash on hand at 17th December, 1891.........   893,491 27
Less outstanding warrants, do 149,600 21   743,891 06

and being the amount remaining of the $3,707,530 proceeds of the loan for 20,000,000 francs and other receipts ($2,073,000 of the Temporary Loans unpaid at the 30th June, 1891, having been paid from the same).

   The Treasury was indebted at the same date for:

Temporary Loans .... $ 150,000 00
Railway Guarantee Deposits 1,860,766 98
Trust Deposits...   265,376 65

   $2,276,143 63

The funded debt of the Province at this date was............ $26,214,353 34

Of the above balance of cash at 17th December............ $743,891 06

the following sums are only available for the special purpose for which they are deposited :—

Special Deposits in Banks, part of Railway
   Guarantee Deposits 387,563 67
Deposits to secure advances by Banks to
   Railway Companies 64,130 00
Special Deposits in Banks not payable until
   after 1st January 75,000 00

   526,693 67

   Leaving available for immediate expenditure.................$217,197 39

This has all been expended for ordinary services and railway subsidies which were due and payable, and there is still an amount of $2,276,143.63 owing for Railway Guarantee and Trust Deposits and Temporary Loans.

   This, as I have said, is not a complete criterion of what the result may be at the end of the year, but is given to show the result of the cash operations up to the date when the Hon. Mr. Shehyn left office.

   The estimates for the whole of the year, as revised, I will give as soon as I have disposed of the loan of about $4,000,000 00.

THE LOAN OF $4,000,000.00.

During this period, as above shown, a portion of the $10,000,000 loan authorized by 54 Vic., Cap. 2 (December 1890) was floated. The loan was for 20,000,000 francs, or $4,000,000, and floated in Paris. 40,000 regular bonds of the Province for 500 francs each bearing date 15th July, 1891, and redeemable in Paris two years from date with half-yearly interest coupons attached at the rate of four per cent. per annum, have been issued. The bonds were placed on the market at 490 francs each, but a commission of 9 francs and 75 centimes, on each bond was paid to the Credit Lyonnais and the Banque de Paris et des Pays-Bas for floating them. This left to the Province 480 francs 25 centimes per 500 franc bond. The proceeds and expenses have been as follows :—

PROCEEDS OF LOAN :

20,000.000 francs at 19 $\frac{3}{5}$ c. per franc............................	3,860,000 00
Sold at Fr. 480.25 per 500 Francs [3·95 per cent. discount]..	152,470 00
19,210,000 francs at credit of Province in Paris 16th August, 1891...	$3,707,530 00

EXPENSES :

Stamps on Bonds	$ 5,790 00	
Printing and Engraving Bonds ·················	965 00	
Insurance and Freight on Bonds...............	96 50	
Loss in Exchange to date........................	14,016 72	
Travelling Expenses	8,802 24	
		29,670 46

The Province also pay a commission of one half per cent for the payments of the coupons and a commission of one quarter per cent for the redemption of the principal if the loan is not merged into and made to form part of the balance of $6,000,000 00.

The loan cannot be said to be advantageous, but is onerous for the Province.

No business man would justify it, nor the expense of issuing regular bonds for a loan of such a short date. As to interest, the Province loses one month's advantage of the proceeds from 16th July to 16th August, when we got the money, and as a matter of fact, taking in the expenses, we are paying 6¼ per cent.

There can be no question such an amount could have been obtained more advantageously from our Banks here for such a period of time.

To finish the year 1891-92 I must tell you frankly our position.

1891–1692.

SUMMARY OF ESTIMATES OF RECEIPTS AND EXPENDITURE OF THE PROVINCE OF QUEBEC FOR THE FISCAL YEAR 1891-92 AS REVISED FROM OFFICIAL REPORTS OF THE DIFFERENT DEPARTMENTS.

RECEIPTS.

Ordinary Receipts as estimated by the Hon. J. Shehyn, Treasurer, in his Budget Speech, 5th December, 1890...................		$3,567,435 70
From this is to be deducted the amount which it is estimated the revenue from Crown Lands will fall short of the Treasurer's estimate		250,000 00
		$3,317,485 70
And to it may be added the following sums which it is estimated will be received over and above the Treasurer's estimate :		
Interest on Deposits, etc.........	25,211 57	
Administration of Justice......	7,734 19	
Licenses	50,000 00	
Direct Taxes......................	4,000 00	
		86,945 76
		$3,404,381 46
On account of which has been received to 17th December, 1891		1,526,498 12
Leaving to be received between the 17th December, 1891, and 30th June, 1892......		$ 1,877,883 34

EXPENDITURE.

Ordinary Expenditure as estimated by the Treasurer in the same Budget Speech......		$3,558,894 79
To this is to be added the following amounts estimated as being required in addition for the following services during the year, viz. :--		
Interest on Public Debt...............	$154,400 00	
Interest on Temporary Loans and Deposits..	3,500 00	

Charges of Management, Public Debt.........	35,671 00	
Legislation..	8,000 00	
Civil Government	16,200 00	
Administration of Justice......................	102,221 41	
Reformatory Prisons and Schools	41,000 00	
Rents, Insurances and Repairs, Public Buildings	25,000 00	
Repairs of Court House and Gaols	18,000 00	
Lunatic Asylums	60,783 65	
Crown Lands......................................	86,000 00	
Miscellaneous Services...........................	15,709 85	
		$556,490 91
		$4,115,385 70
On account of which there has been paid to 17th December, 1891...........................		2,097,925 32
Leaving to be paid between the 17th Dec. 1891 and 30th June, 1892....................		$ 2,017,460 38

SPECIAL EXPENDITURE.

The Treasurer's estimated Special Expenditure for the same period was................		$ 1,826,581 39
To which is to be added the following amounts estimated as being required in addition for the following services during the year, viz. :		
Montreal Court House Extension...............	$ 180,000 00	
Jacques Cartier Normal School..................	29,757 90	
McGill Normal School	6,580 00	
Railway subsidies................................	214,771 95	
		431,109 85
		$ 2,257,691 24
On account of which has been paid to 17th December........		566,406 48
Leaving to be paid between the 17th December, 1891, and 30th June, 1892...................................		$ 1,691,284 76

The above estimates, as revised, show that the result of the financial operations for the year 1891-92 will be as follows :

Estimated ordinary receipts, as revised......	3,404,381 46	
Estimated ordinary expenditure, as revised	4,115,385 70	
Deficit of ordinary revenue to meet ordinary expenditure		711,004 24
Estimated special expenditures, as revised..	$2,257,691 24	
Estimated special receipts........................	3,000 00	
		2,254,691 24
Excess of expenditure over revenue during 1891-92		$2,965,695 48

It is possible, however, that of the Special Expenditure, though the items have been voted, $300,000.00 or $400,000.00 may not be called for during the current year.

II.

ASSETS AND LIABILITIES.

An examination of our assets and liabilities on 31st January, 1887, when my predecessor took over affairs, and on the 17th December 1891, when he left office, taken in connection with the accounts and figures I have just given you, will show very clearly what the result of the administration has been and how enormously our debt has been increased. In fact it has been more than doubled within the last 4½ years.

Mr. Shehyn had a statement of the assets and liabilities made up on 31 January, 1887, and since that date they have been made up on the 30th June in each year and I have them made up on the 17th December 1891.

I might go back to the 30th June 1886, the last year of the Ross-Taillon administration and show you that the difference was very much greater, but, as time is important, I will take the assets and liabilities during Mr. Shehyn's regime.

The following then is a summary of the assets and liabilities at various dates as given since the 31st January, 1887, down to the 17th December, 1891.

SUMMARY.

ASSETS AND LIABILITIES.

1887, January 31st—Liabilities		$22,143,447 65
Assets		10,754,280 54
Net debt...		$11,389,167 11

1887, June 30th—Liabilities	$22,188,700	08
Assets...	10,859,069	10
Net debt...............	$11,329,620	98
1888, June 30th—Liabilities	$24,180,461	56
Assets	12,284,969	49
Net debt..........	$11,895,492	07
1889, June 30th—Liabilities	$27,157,808	21
Assets	12,813,960	50
Net debt............	$14,343,847	71
1890, June 30th—Liabilities	$27,186,852	25
Assets	11,131,785	14
Net debt...........	$16,055,067	11
1891, June 30th—Liabilities	$34,888,207	05
Assets.............	11,139,553	30
Net debt.............	$23,748,653	75
1891, December 17th—Liabilities	$35,984,875	60
Assets................	11,561,191	98
Net debt........	$24,423,683	62

It would take too long to give the details for these various years, though I have them with me here to-night. I will give, however, first the statement of the assets and liabilities at the 31st January, 1887, as made up under Mr. Shehyn. In this he makes it as favorable as possible for himself and charges up against his predecessors every liability he could.

APPROXIMATE STATEMENT OF LIABILITIES AND ASSETS OF THE PROVINCE OF QUEBEC AT 31ST JANUARY, 1887:

LIABILITIES.

Funded debt outstanding...	$18,155,013	33
Temporary loans and deposits.....................................	729,227	67
Outstanding warrants at 31st January, 1887	16,196	78

Estimated deficiency of revenue of current year 1886-87 to meet expenditure, not including payments to be made on railway subsidies. Parliament buildings. Q. M. O. & O. Ry. construction claims and Quebec Court House 370,842 06

Railway money subsidies authorized, but not yet earned ... 579,732 25

Railway land subsidies converted into money subsidies under 49-50 Vic., cap. 77, and authorized by Order-in-Council prior to the 31st January, 1887, 3,800,500 acres at 70 cts. per acre....................... $ 2,660,350 00

First 35 cts. per acre payable as the work is done .... $ 1,330,175 00
Paid on account of same to 31st January, 1887 .... 245,846 50
                                                                                             1,084,328 50

Railway land subsidies which may be converted into money subsidies, 1,326,000 acres at 70 cents per acre .... $ 928,200 00

First 35 cts. per acre payable as the work is done.............. $ 464,100 00

Estimated cost of completing Parliament buildings :—

Admitted claim for work done to 31st January .... $ 90,000 00
Estimated amount required to complete..... 115,113 91
                                                                                             205,113 91

Contract for statues on Parliament buildings 25,000 00

Estimated cost of completing Quebec Court House :—

Admitted claims for work done to 31st January............... .... $ 70,000 00
Estimated amount required to complete 152,823 15
                                                                                             222,823 15

Balance of land and other debts Q. M. O. & O. Ry............   64,070 00
Loss on Exchange Bank deposit 27,000 00
Quebec Court House Bonds.....................................   200,000 00

                                                                                          $22,143,447 65

ASSETS.

Part of price of Q. M. O. & O. Ry. deposited in banks............ .... $	400,000 00	
Part of price of Q. M. O. & O. Ry. invested in Quebec Court House bonds..............	200,000 00	
Balance of price of Q. M. O. & O. Ry. remaining unpaid............	7,000,000 00	
		$ 7,600,000 00
Capitalized railway subsidies under Dominion Act 47 Vic., cap. 8.............,.....		2,894,000 00
Special deposit in La Banque Jacques Cartier, payment of which has been refused on account of counter claim in re Hon. Thomas McGreevy..		100,000 00
Cash in banks..		11,473 00
Cost of Jacques Cartier School, Montreal, to be repaid from sale of property..		138,348 02
Advance to various parties .... $	88,271 40	
Estimated amount due as interest on Common School fund from Ontario..............	100,000 00	
		188,271 40
City of Montreal, subscription to Hull bridge...............		50,000 00
City of Montreal, contribution towards land expropriated between Hochelaga and Dalhousie Square		72,138 02
Quebec Court House tax under 45 Vic., cap. 26, and 48 Vic., cap. 15........		200,000 00
		$10,754.280 54
Excess of liabilities over assets at 31st January, 1887.........		11,389,167 11
		$22,143,447 65

Treasury Department,
Quebec, 30th March, 1887,   H. T. MACHIN,
                                             Assistant Treasurer P.Q.

Passing over the details on the 30th June following in each year, I come to the 17th December, 1891, and give the details, and the public will see the enormous and startling difference and increase.

APPROXIMATE STATEMENT OF LIABILITIES AND ASSETS OF THE PROVINCE OF QUEBEC AT 17TH DECEMBER, 1891.

LIABILITIES.

Funded debt outstanding..	$25,209,873	33
Temporary loans..	150,000	00
Trust deposits..	258,243	25
Railway Company deposits to meet guaranteed interest on bonds	1,860,765	64
Outstanding warrants...	149,600	21
Railway money subsidies authorized, but not yet carned $3,147,910 99		
Railway land subsidies converted into money subsidies authorized, but not earned—balance on first 35c per acre 2,595,836 00		
Railway land subsidies, which may be converted into money subsidies, 4,638,000 acres at 70c per acre........................$3,246,600 00		
First 35c per acre, payable as work is done... 1,623,300 00		
	7,867,046	99
Balance of land and other grants Q. M. O. &O. Ry............	51,99J	73
Special expenditure for 1891-92 under the Act 54 Vic., cap. 1, sch. B.............................$ 888,555 00		
Less paid on account to 17th December, 1891.. 128,208 55		
	710,346	45
Loss on Exchange Bank deposit	27,000	00
Quebec Court House bonds	200,000	00
	$35,934,875	60

ASSETS.

Part of price Q. M. O. & O. Ry. deposited in banks............$	853,390	00
Part of price Q. M. O. & O. Ry. invested in $29,000.00 Province of Quebec Bonds, loan of 1878, bought at 109 p.c...	31,610	00
Part of price Q. M. O. & O. Ry. invested in Quebec Court House Bonds...................	200,000	00

Part of price Q M. O. & O.
Ry. invested in City of Que-
bec Bonds....................... 15,000 00
Balance of price of Q. M. O. &
O. Ry. unpaid................. 7,000,000 00
————— $ 7,600,000 00
Railway grant under Dominion Act 47 Vic.,
cap. 8 .... 2,394,000 00
Cash in banks................................. 893,491 27
Claim against Hon. Thomas McGreevy...... 100,000 00
Cost of Jacques Cartier School, Montreal, to
be repaid from sale of property.............. 138,348 02
Advances to various parties..................... 145,352 69
Estimated amount due as Quebec's share of
interest on Common School fund from
Ontario 90,000 00
Quebec Court House tax under 45 Vic., cap.
26 and 48 Vic., cap 15 .... 200,000 00
————— $11,561,191 98
Excess of liabilities over assets at 17th December, 1891...... 24,423.683 62

$35,984,875 60

Note.—This excess of liabilities is exclusive of $714,004.24, estimated
deficiency of ordinary revenue to meet ordinary expenditure during the
fiscal year ending 30th June, 1892.

TREASURY DEPARTMENT,
    QUEBEC, 9th January, 1892.   H. T. MACHIN,
                                         Assistant Treasurer.

III.

THE ADMINISTRATION UNDER HON. MR. MERCIER'S REGIME.

This is my last heading, and the statements here will well justify the
charge of reckless and extravagant administration.

Turning again to Mr. Shehyn's speech of 1887 (at page 65) on this
head he said, " Lastly, our well defined policy, one of the principal features
of our programme, is to exercise the strictest supervision over the expenditure of the public moneys, to closely watch their outlay, to control all the
expenses, and to conduct the business of the Province as the business of

our best managed financial institutions and great commercial houses are conducted, and according to the rules and the practice observed in these institutions.

" This is the end we have in view. To attain it, however, we must necessarily take time to seriously and thoroughly study all the details of our administrative organization so as to avoid doing anything that may not be in keeping with prudence and that will not produce solid and lasting results. I am quite convinced that, by acting with discernment and in accordance with the principles of a wise administrative economy, we shall succeed in materially and permanently reducing our ordinary and controllable expenses."

This was assuring, and it is well to bear it in mind in view of the following figures.

The expenditure in connection with the Province has been made under the following heads :

Public Debt,	Public Works,
Legislation,	Asylums,
Civil Government,	Charities,
Justice,	Miscellaneous Services,
Public Instruction,	Special Expenditure,
Agriculture,	Railways,
Colonization and Immigration.	

My first statement will be then to show you, as a preliminary one, the various estimates made by Mr. Shehyn in his Budget Speeches during the years for which he was responsible, and how far he was wrong in each one of his calculations. This will prepare you to a certain extent for the other figures I will give you. I will ask you again to bear in mind, when I mention *a year* it means the year ending 30th June :—

	Estimates.	Expenditures.
1888	$4,220,736 00	$4,675,077 20
1889	4,175,222 86	4,994,590 22
1890	4,889,024 44	5,003,591 86
1891	4,877,828 24	5.817,678 48

The detailed statement of these estimates and expenditures and under which the estimates are made, is found in the annexed statement " A."

I will now come to the heads of expenditure, under the headings above mentioned and give throughout, the expenditure in 1886, the last year of the Ross-Taillon administration.

EXPENDITURE ON ACCOUNT OF PUBLIC DEBT.

1886 including	$51,994 25	of bonds redeemed....................	$ 977,760 82
1887 "	54,359 44	" "	.... 1,016,022 14
1888 "	56,845 10	" "	.... 1,103,710 94
1889 "	59,429 29	" "	.... 1,134,789 51
1890 "	62,133 95	" "	.... 1.259,406 88
1891 "	64,970 00	" "	.... 1,271,506 83

The detals of this are in the annexed Statement B.

In the details of the Public Debt, there are one or two startling items in connection with interest on the unfunded debt, which includes, of course, interest on temporary loans, and is a fair criterion of administrative ability in carrying on the affairs of any business, and much more so, the affairs of the Province of Quebec. Now let us see what has been paid for interest on temporary loans and unfunded debt during the various years :

1886......................	$ 26,846 68
1887..	67,038 92
1888..	75,228 10
1889..	39,525 88
1890..	149,741 40
1891..	170,787 23

It will thus be seen that this Province was paying about $171,000 for interest on ordinary operations during the last financial year, and these figures will be interesting to show later on how far some economy might be made in the administration.

Let us take another item in connection with the public debt, that is, the item of Commission, Stamps, etc. Here are the amounts paid as follows :—

1886......................	$ 5,081 22
1887...... ....,....	5,074 93
1888......................	13,438 44
1889..	7,339 42
1890...	24,021 40
1891..	14,588 25

It is sometimes difficult to trace and ferret out what these various amounts are actually paid for. Of course, in the year 1888 there is a reason for the increase on account of the loan of three millions and a half negotiated in that year, but in the year 1890 there can be no justification for such a large amount of $24,021.50.

There is one item in that year of $13,000 mentioned in the public accounts as paid to La Banque du Peuple for fees and disbursements in connection with the management of the public debt. This item is for a sum of $13,000 not paid to La Banque du Peuple but paid to Mr. C. Beausoleil for his so-called commission in the negotiation of the loan of three millions and a half. Strange to say this loan was made in the early part of 1888 and, for the first time, and without there being any record at all in the department, or any correspondence to show Mr. Beausoleil is entitled to anything, this sum of $13,000 is falsely entered as a payment to La Banque du Peuple.

We have the Public Accounts for 1888 and for 1889, yet not a word about this account. Why was it suppressed for two years? However, this is nothing but a suspicious and delusive entry. On the 28th June, 1889, Mr. Beausoleil made his final return of collections of the taxes on commercial corporations. According to his statement he had collected $521,041 93. Among other items he claimed a commission of 2½ per cent. or $13,041 93 which he deducted and paid over the balance. The same day Mr. Shehyn acknowledged receipt and thanked Mr. Beausoleil for the manner in which he had collected the tax and performed his duty to the satisfaction of the Government.

The same day, 28th June, 1889, Mr Shehyn wrote a letter of credit to Mr. Beausoleil that "the Government would pay Mr. Beausoleil early in " July the sum of $13,000 for the latter's fees, disbursements, etc., in con- " nection with the loan of 1887."

Mr. Beausoleil then presented his account for services in connection with the loan, amounting to $13,041.92. He was paid $13,000 by discounting the letter of credit with La Banque du Peuple. When the $13,000 was paid by the Government, to hide it up they entered it as paid La Banque du Peuple. It will be seen, however, it was just one way to pay M Beausoleil 5 per cent. on his collection of the corporation tax, and deceive the public, as the item in connection with the loan is the same amount as the 2½ per cent. deducted.

LEGISLATION.

The next item we come to is that of Legislation. Now this item in-cludes the expenses of the Legislative Assembly and of the Legislative Council, of the library and the expenses of elections. If there is any item more than another that can be controlled by the Government it is this one, but here are the expenses under this heading for the various years:—

1886	$181,987 75
1887	278,169 07
1888	228,994 88
1889	231,912 90
1890	312,948 81
1891	281,078 74

I give the details of these expenditures in the statement " C.," and a glance at this will show where the great increase is, and it will be seen that for the Legislative Council and the Legislative Assembly the figures are as follows :—

1886	$160,810 34
1887	199,452 09
1888	195,065 32
1889	203,279 49
1890	282,492 50
1891	247,808 62

There is then a difference under this heading alone which has no possible reason or justification, as there is nothing to show any greater satisfaction to the people, of $87,000 odd from the last session held under the Ross-Taillon administration, and that of the last session held under the Mercier administration.

CIVIL GOVERNMENT.

Under this heading are the ordinary expenses of the departments at Quebec and their agencies in carrying on the business of the Province. The figures run as follows :—

1886	$183,675 41
1887	193,904 06
1888	208,677 61
1889	236,987 39
1890	255,144 20
1891	269,660 07

These figures are divided under two heads, what is called departmental salaries and the other insidious word " contingencies." The figures under the head of Departmental Salaries are as follows :—

1886	$138,328 32
1887	144,896 84
1888	153,652 25
1889	175,099 89
1890	188,494 20
1891	202,480 07

CONTINGENCIES.

1886 ....$	40,658 61
1887	43,960 02
1888 ...... :	40,715 87
1889	57,581 73
1890	63,135 20
1891	61,780 97

Then a further sub-division has been made :—

SPECIAL CONTINGENCIES.

1886 ....$	4 188 48
1887	4,547 20
1888	4,809 99
1889	3,705 77
1890	3,014 80
1891	4,799 03

I have nothing to add to these figures. The public must judge how much better or worse we have been governed the last four years and how far this great increase can be excused, or how far administrative ability has been called into play. Statement D annexed shews the details.

ADMINISTRATION OF JUSTICE.

Now we come to the next heading—that is, Administration of Justice.

Before going into the figures of this head I will again quote from Mr. Shehyn's speech of the 12th April, 1887, and in which, after criticising his predecessors, he says, about their administration :—

" I think it possible to inaugurate reforms in the administration of " Justice, and considerably reduce the cost of that service. My hon. " friend, the Premier, is giving his attention to this important question, " and, I am justified in saying, will not fail to deal successfully with it " when he shall have the necessary time at his disposal after the session."

Now, I will show you that this was but a vain promise, and, instead, we have not only had lack of supervision and lack of enquiry into these expenses, but they have gone on and increased in a manner that is almost scandalous, and here are the figures :—

1886	$478,506 08
1887......................	497,309 23
1888......................	454,146 07
1889......................................	559,120 46
1890......................................	599,883 50
1891......................................	679,006 18

I have submitted a statement ("E") to show the details of the expenditure under this head. An examination of that will show that, while there has been possibly an ordinary and fair increase in salaries and other matters, owing to increase of business, yet, under headings of Contingencies and Miscellaneous matter, the increase challenges more than inspection and invites suspicion.

Let us take one particular heading, that is, of payments, the contingent expenses of the Sheriffs. This is over and beyond all salaries, and the details of it are well worth reading :—

SHERIFFS' CONTINGENCIES.

1886	$160.626 84
1887	169,203 14
1888	212.868 97
1889	212,591 36
1890	226.364 52
1891	283,999 35

or, as a result under this item alone, of which I cannot conceive any justication for, there has been an annual enormous increase, and for the last year these contingent expenses were $123,372 51 more than they were for the year 1866. I can only say that these expenses and this increase seem to me alarming.

Let us take the other heading, of " Miscellaneous Justice," and, of course, for business or practical men, these words contingencies and miscellaneous always sound dangerous.

This item is supposed to represent the costs, fees and expenses in various suits or matters that may come up in which the Government may be interested. This interest is very often determined by the desire of the administration to interfere in suits or give patronage to their friends. Here are the figures under this item :—

MISCELLANEOUS JUSTICE.

1886	$ 6,185 56
1887	9,383 40
1888	1<,195 94
1889	28,031 21
1890	32,537 96
1891	30,010 40

or a difference last year of $23,°84 84 over the expenditure made the last year of the Ross-Taillou administration. The public themselves will have to decide how far there has been such an amount of miscellaneous justice as to warrant this expenditure, I see none.

In the Legislative Assembly, this expenditure of Administration of Justice has been frequently attacked, but it has been urged against it that the revenue from the Administration of Justice has been very much increased. Let us take the statement of the revenue from the Administration of Justice. It includes law and registration stamps, the result of prison labor, breaking of stones, &c., and the figures of receipts are as follows :—

REVENUE.

1886 ....$219,374 63
1887 .... 202,042 58
1888 .... 252 204 23
1889 .... 214,626 68
1890 .... 226,727 64
1891 .... 236,694 48

I have a detailed statement of this marked " F," but as a general result it will be seen that there is only an increase of receipts of $17,319 85 in 1891 over that in 1886, so that no justification is to be found in these receipts of this immense expenditure,

PUBLIC INSTRUCTION.

The next item is Public Instruction, and here the figures are as follows :

1886 ....$362.122 75
1887 .... 390,901 79
1888 .... 374,959 53
1889 .... 390,835 00
1890 .... 386,485 00
1891 .... 402,106 34

It will be seen that the increase in the expenditure in this worthy object has only been $39,983,58 over that of the last year of the Ross-Taillon administration. To the friends of educational progress in this country and viewing the large sums spent and the large increases in all other departments, it gives a fair indication of what the desires and interests were of the late administration.

AGRICULTURE.

We now come to the expenditure of agriculture. The figures are as follows :—

1886.. $ 79,682.00
1887.. 89,476.00
1888.. 97,700.00
1889.. 94,061.00
1890.. 98,636.00
1891.. 112,737.00

Agriculture is one of the most important interests for this Province, and should have a great deal of attention devoted to it, yet it is seen by the above figures that the increase in five years in this important branch is only about $33,000. Annexed is statement marked G, showing the details.

COLONIZATION.

Coming to the next item of Colonization, which includes Emigration, the figures are as follows :

1886	$170,295 11
1887	163,000 00
1888	94,800 00
1889	131,747 00
1890	151,015 53
1891	182,891 80

Here the increase is very insignificant, and shows how little desirous the late administration were for the real progress of the country. Annexed is a statement marked H showing the details of this service.

PUBLIC WORKS.

Here again we find a very large increase of expense, and Mr. Shehyn in his Public Accounts has divided these into what is called Ordinary and Special. The following is the expenditure under these sub-headings, details being in Statement I :—

ORDINARY.

1886	$ 82,584.40
1887	94,575.94
1888	145,096.91
1889	110,164.23
1890	148,841.23
1891	139,612.83

It has been impossible, with the little time at my disposal to investigate and dissect these increases.

SPECIAL.

Under this heading the following are the figures :—

1886	$177,000.00
1887	395,510.42
1888	530,922.83
1889	297,863.12
1890	315,359.75
1891	678,000.08

In this latter connection of course the great bulk of the expenditure is that in connection with the new Parliament Buildings, the Quebec Court House and the extension to the Montreal Court House. With reference to the two first buildings, an enormous amount of money has been spent on them. When the Mercier administration came into power, these buildings were practically completed, but the dealing with them was in the hands of Mr. McShane, the then Commissioner of Public Works who, fortunately for the country, did not remain long in charge of that department. But before giving you the expenditure made by Mr. Shehyn, I must quote from his speech of the 12th April 1687. He complained bitterly of the expense on these buildings up to that date, and said : " Nevertheless, " this is not all. Work on the Court House has been going on since 1st " February, and the works at the Parliament Buildings will be resumed as " soon as the snow disappears, that is to say they will be carried on during " the two months comprised between the 30th April and the 30th June. " We shall thus have still more to pay for them, in addition to the $157,062.94 " due on the 1st February, in excess of the estimate of the hon. member for " Sherbrooke. According to an estimate prepared with the utmost care by " the architect of the Department of Public Works and by Mr. Lesage, the " Assistant Commi-sioner, the works that will be executed between the 1st " February and the 30th June, 1887, will necessitate an outlay of $52,823.15 " for the Court House and $40,113.91 for the Parliament Buildings, making " a total of $92,397.16, and when this sum is added to the increase of ex- " penses already noted for the 1st February, it will be found that my hon. " friend, the member for Sherbrooke's, estimate for these works $126,120 will " be exceeded by $250,000.00.

" Mr Speaker, let me say that this is rather inexplicable. If my hon. " predecessor did not knowingly and deliberately mislead the House, the " late Government have proof of an incompetence, of a recklessness, which I " cannot refrain from characterizing as inexcusable.

" That there was inexcusable carelessness on the part of our predecessors " in the direction of the undertakings in question we have ascertained " beyond doubt. It is almost incredible, but it is not less the fact that the " works, in both cases were executed partly by contract and partly by the " day, in such a way as to leave the Government in reality at the mercy of " the contractors. This was a most unwarrantable state of things. The " work was done by extras according to the schedules of prices of the ori- " ginal contract, whether upon the estimate of the architect, on the verbal " order of the Commissioner and sometimes even upon the suggestions of the " contractors themselves with regard to certain changes in the original plans " of the buildings. It is consequently not at all astonishing that under such " an irregular system, the contractors should have supplementary claims,

" but happily not admitted, amounting to $316,000 over and above the enor-
" mous amounts with regard to which there can be no question, since they
" have been admitted by our predecessors on the certificates of the depart-
" mental architect."

And he also says :—

"The statements supplied by the officers of the Public Works and
" Treasury Departments establish that, when completed, the Quebec Court
" House will cost $528,210.71, and the Parliament Buildings $579,984.14. A
" comparison of these figures with the prices stipulated in the original con-
" tracts gives the following results :—

" COURT HOUSE.

" Cost of work, as above established............................	$528,210 71
" Cost of work according to contract, as established at page	
223 or the report of the commissioner of Public	
Works for 1883..	135,000 00
" Excess of real price over contract price parliament buildings	
" Cost of work as above established............................	570,584 14
" Price of work according to contract as established at page	
223 of the Report of the Commissioner of Public	
Works for 1883	185,160 84

" As will be seen, the two buildings were to have cost according to
" the original contracts $320,160 84, but, thanks to the unpardonable care-
" lessness with which the works were supervised and directed by our pre-
" decessors, these two undertaking are going to cost $1,107,794 95 of $786,634,
" 21 more than their contract price.

" I ask you in all sincerity Mr. Speaker, whether it was possible to give
" more absolute proof of want of competence and administrative capacity.'

These were the expressions of Mr. Shehyn's indignation, but let us see
how far they were feigned or what recklessness and incompetency ensued?

Of course the Hon. Mr. McShane was Commissioner of Public Works,
and this Mr. Shehyn never counted upon. But let us see what the Mercier administration did with these buildings ? Remember, they were practically completed when Hon. Mr. Mercier came into power. The Legislature voted Mr. Shehyn in 1887, all the money that he said he wanted for the purposes of completing them and for the year ending the 30th
June, 1887. After that date Mr. Shehyn was responsible for all the money
spent, and here is what was spent :—

NEW PARLIAMENT BUILDINGS.

1888	$ 250,000 00
1889	125,729 53
1890	162,760 00
1891	18,495 34
Total	$551,934 87

and that building is not yet completed.

Let us now look at the amount spent on the Quebec Court House :

1888	$ 210,000 00
1889	42,788 59
1890	49,037 36
1891	159,007 00
Total	$460,779 05

It will therefore be seen that on these two structures alone, and after the Mercier administration came into power, they have spent $1,012,764, though the buildings were practically completed, and notwithstanding over and above this sum there was voted in 1887 the sum of $92,897 18.

It is a fair example of the way contracts and works have been done in the Province of Quebec under the Mercier administration. A great portion of these works were done without contract, and even, in some cases, without the Department knowing what was going on.

ASYLUMS.

The expenditure under this head has been as follows :

1886	$230,000 00
1887	248,000 00
1888	241,000 00
1889	230,000 00
1890	230,000 00
1891	269,143 33

The increase here does not seem very large, and may be a natural increase, as it covers a period of five years.

I have not had time to investigate it.

CHARITIES.

The following are the figures :—

1886	$37,716 00
1887	39,316 00
1888	39,316 00
1889	41,996 00
1890	44,306 00
1891	47,739 33

These figures require no comment.

MISCELLANEOUS SERVICES.

1886	$197,030 40
1887	495,510 42
1888	637,768 76
1889	397,638 40
1890	818,483 51
1891	820,254 15

This is one of the most difficult classes of expenditure to unravel or give you any sort of intelligent idea about. Practically speaking, all classes of expenditure being put in at one time or another by Mr. Shehyn under this head.

I have divided it into two heads :—

1. Expense of Collection of Revenue.
2. Miscellaneous Payments.

Under the first head are included :

The General Expenditure of Crown Lands outside the Department, Municipalities Fund, *Official Gazette*, Stamps, Odd Licenses, Inspection of Railways, Payment by Revenue Officers, &c. The following are the figures :—

1886	$191,080 13
1887	210,269 83
1888	207,177 50
1889	284,031 85
1890	315,150 08
1891	367,961 72

I have given a detail of this annexed as Statement K. The increase is not justifiable or excusable. A large portion appears in the Crown Lands Department outside service, to which I will allude later on. But, on examining the payments by Revenue officers, it will be seen their expenses or payments, which are very questionable, are increased almost double.

Under the second head of Miscellaneous Services are included :— Printing and distributing books, pamphlets, &c., commissions, arbitrations, enquiries and conferences, transcription of registers, documents, &c., special and extra services by various parties, grants, &c., to exhibitions, advocates and notaries for professional services, aid to distressed parties and sufferers by fire, aid to institutions, societies, bridges, &c., civil service pensions and teachers pensions, travelling expenses of certain parties, agent in France, &c., &c. The figures for these also shows alarming increases :—

1886	....$	57,800	00
1887	....	72,793	50
1888	....	68,952	87
1889	....	93,112	37
1890	....	79,955	18
1891	....	122,086	69

The growth of literature and pamphlets in the past two years has been enormous.

In the year 1890-91 we have paid $52,854 03 for this service and it will be hard to ascertain where any return is.

SPECIAL EXPENDITURE, (exclusive of Railways).

1886	....	$197,080	40
1887	....	495,510	42
1888	....	637,767	76
1889	....	397,638	40
1890	....	818,583	51
1891	....	820,254	15

This is a head of expenditure created by Mr. Shehyn and includes repairs to public buildings, heating apparatuses for court houses and gaols, expenditure for iron bridges, for night schools, codification of the laws, special explorations in different counties, expenses of arbitration between Quebec and Ontario, settlement of Lockwood's claim, Speaker's portraits, library late Judge Polette, new vaults in court houses and gaols, general index Journals of Legislative Assembly, damages by wind storms in counties of Beauharnois, Vaudreuil and Huntingdon, colonization roads, etc., etc. The full details I have given before in the statements of the cash operations each year. But the total result of it all is, an enormous expenditure under that heading, and which Mr. Shehyn puts there in order to conceal to a large extent the expenses that should be ordinary expenses. Mr. Shehyn, in his 1887 speech, criticised Mr. Robertson's classification of ordinary and extraordinary expenditure, and he (Mr. Shehyn) in defining these expenditures, said :

" I have included in the ordinary expenses a sum of $100,000 applied
" to Colonization Roads. This sum, although specified in the Budget, has
" been taken from a loan, really falls into the category of ordinary expenses.
" It is quite true that it is exceptional on account of its figures, but not so on
" account of its use, since expenses of this nature occurred each year." An examination of Mr. Shehyn's subsequent classification of the accounts show how lightly he considered his criticism of Mr. Robertson and how insincere were his declarations. In looking at the various items under this head as

given in the statements of cash, it is quite clear many, if not practically all, should be classed as ordinary expense. Most of them, to use Mr. Shehyn's words, are recurrent. It was convenient, however, to put them under this head so as to try and make a good showing in the ordinary expenses, but in the end, of course, it only deceived the people.

RAILWAYS.

This is the last item of expenditure, which is as follows:

1886	$ 322,970 82
1887	744,896 70
1888	662,275 30
1889	1,076,647 00
1890	848,417 97
1891	955,620 26

The expenditure under this heading now has much more importance, owing to the recent revelations that have come out before the Royal Commission of the Baie des Chaleurs Railway, and before the second Royal Commission recently appointed. There is one thing evident at the present moment, that large portions of these railway subsidies have not gone for the purposes intended by the Legislature. On the contrary, large portions have been found divided up between members of the late Government and Mr. Pacaud, and received by them for their personal and political advantage.

CROWN LANDS.

Before closing this question of administration, under this heading that I have given, there is another department of very serious importance to the Province, that is, the Department of Crown Lands. It is one of our great sources of assets, but I regret to say that it is one in which the most shameless and disgraceful administration, according to the Public Accounts, has existed during the past few years. It will be borne in mind, also, that on the 7th April, 1887, the dues from timber limits were increased from $2 to $5 an acre, giving an additional revenue of from at least $140,000 to $150,000 a year. Two sales of timber limits have taken place within the short period of four years of the late administration, the receipts from these sales being as follows:

Total price sale 17th October, 1888		$140,825 74
Of which paid 1889	$118,097 99	
Paid 1891	6,060 00	
Balance still due	16,667 75	
		140,825 74

Sale 9th January, 1890 yielded $157,679 12
Of which paid 1890 ....   27,128 07
Paid 1891..   6,595 00
Balance still due......................................   133,956 05
                                                                          157,679 12

I will now give you the figures in order that you may judge for your-
selves. I will give you the revenue and the expenses side by side.

	Revenue	Expenses.
1886	$620.821 76	$178.974 16
1887	692.620 48	202.427 50
1888	725.627 50	236,456 18
1889	1,075,045 42	255,591 63
1890	918,627 77	297,744 59
1881	742,544 62	353,518 39

I don't know that any words could express adequately a comment on
the last year. It will be seen that it cost 50 per cent. to collect, and com-
paring it with 1885-86, it would evidently have been far better for the
Province to have had no further increase of taxation. In order that there
may be no doubt I give you statements annexed, J, showing the details
of this. The statement also includes the expenses of the Department at
Quebec already included in the heading of Civil Government. They are
as follows, and deducted from the above will show the expenses outside
the Department.

1886	$48.974 16
1887	48,316 50
1888	51,861 25
1889	54,891 63
1890	57,912 39
1891	65,643 89

This covers the question of administration, and it does seem to me
that the figures given you above show absolute proof, not only of incompetency, but on account of the extensive nature of the expenses, indicate
that they have been reckless and corrupt. A few more years of administration of that kind and the Province will be done.

It will be seen, as a brief summary, and taking Mr. Shehyn's own
figures from the Public Accounts between his administration and the prior
Ross-Taillon administration, there is the following annual increase in the
administration under the following heads :—

Interest on Current affairs...................................	$143,940 55
Legislation	99,090 92
Civil Government...	85,463 06
Administration of Justice...................................	200,500 10
Forming a total of..	$703,034 29

Now, if we take into consideration the items under Special Ependiture and Miscellaneous Services and other matters of the kind which, in former years, were charged to ordinary and departmental expenses, it will be found that the yearly cost of administering the affairs of this Province have increased between the Mercier administration and that of its predecessors by a sum exceeding one million dollars a year up to the 30th June, 1891, and if we add to it then the interest on the new loan of $10,000,000, we will find that the annual burden has been increased $1,500,000 00 at the very least.

LETTERS OF CREDIT.

It is one of the great principles of the British Constitution that no public monies can be expended unless previously voted by the Legislature; the representatives of the people, and the Province should never be bound excepting by such a vote. This rule suffers, however, one exception, with reference to unforeseen expenditure, and the money necessary for any such may be authorized by what is called a Special Warrant. This involves a report from the Minister in charge of the Department where the expenditure is going to take place, being submitted to Council and approved of by Council, and subsequently approved of by the Lieutenant-Governor. Thereupon a Special Warrant may issue, signed by the Lieutenant-Governor, to meet the payment referred to. The late Mercier administration have violated persistently and openly the constitution in issuing letters of credit. The credit of the Province has been injured and obligations have been incurred through the issue of letters of credit signed from time to time either by the First Minister or by the individual Ministers themselves, without in any way having made any report to the Executive Council, or having been approved of in any way by the Lieutenant-Governor. It is elementary to conclude that such a course would have but one result, that would be, ruining the credit of the Province, and throwing upon the Province obligations contracted at the will of an individual Minister. Such a policy cannot be sanctioned and must be absolutely condemned. Were it to receive any sort of sanction from the people it would easily be seen how the Province might be ruined if each Minister could bind it for practically any amount by means of letters of credit. This system of issuing letters of credit by the Mercier administration was frequently attacked in the Legislature, and more particularly on the 1st April, 1890, as appears by the Journals of the House for that year, page 504. A vote of censure was moved and couched in the following words :—

" That the system followed on a most extensive scale by the present " Government, and consisting in issuing letters or documents generally " known as letters of credit is a serious attack upon the power and privi-

" lege of this House of controlling the expenditure of public money, while
" at the same time it disregards the authority of the Crown represented by
" His Honour the Lieutenant-Governor ;
   " That this House deems it its duty, to point, amongst other things,
" certain facts in this connection which have come to their knowledge and
" which are of a nature to show the abuses committed by the present Gov-
" ernment in this respect especially."
   Then the facts in connection with Letters of Credit were given as
follows :—

PUBLIC WORKS DEPARTMENT.

From 1st January, 1889, to 24th February, 1890, for.............. $122,675 56

CROWN LANDS DEPARTMENT.

Acceptance of accounts...	20,900 70
For surveys..	34,787 00
For cadastral services rendered by Forest Rangers and other services	70,161 74
Total...	$248,525 00

This motion, however, was voted down.

   This injurious system has still increased, and at the time of the dismissal of the Mercier Administration, and when I took office, I asked the
various Banks for a statement of all Letters of Credit, promises to pay,
guarantees or acknowledgments which they might have, and consider as
claims against the Province. The details of all these are included in the
Proclamation appointing the Commission to investigate the matter and
amount altogether to over $180.000. They include, of course, the famous
Langlais letters for stationery, and for the purchase of the book called " La
Sylviculteur," yet in connection with this large sum for which the credit
of the Province is sought to be affected, not one cent has been voted by
the House, and they are all obligations contracted by the act of the separate
Ministers, without the authority of an Order-in-Council.
   In addition to the letters of credit, other important letters have been
given, and more particularly one by Mr. Garneau. In February, 1891,
Mr Garneau gave a letter to Mr. Phillippe Valliere of Quebec, giving Mr.
Valliere the opportunity to supply all the furniture and fittings of the
present McGill Normal School, in course of construction ; for the present
Montreal Court House, now being repaired, and for all the furniture and
fittings of the Montreal Gaol, which has not even yet been commenced.
This letter is a singular document ; it contains no prices, or list of prices,

for the fittings and furniture to be supplied by Mr. Valliere, nor their extent or nature. Still, more strange to say, that it must be evidence of the corrupt nature of this letter, Mr. Garneau kept it in his pocket from February, 1891, to the 17th December, 1891, when he relinquished his office. During the whole period of that time there is no record of it whatever in the Department.

EXPENSE.

I might also, as another illustration, give you an idea of the recklessness of the late administration, and might take the travelling expenses in connection with the various public loans and other matters.

STATEMENT SHOWING AMOUNTS PAID FOR TRAVELLING EXPENSES OF DIFFERENT PERSONS IN CONNECTION WITH THE NEGOTIATION OF THE VARIOUS LOANS OF THE PROVINCE.

LOAN OF 1874.

1874.
June 9—Hon. J. G. Robertson's expenses to England $ 591 64

LOAN OF 1876.

1876.
June 9—Hon. L. R. Church's expenses to England.. $ 300 00
Dec. 1—   Do   bal.   do   ..   1,050 55
                                           $1,350 55

LOAN OF 1878.

1879.
Feb. 28—Hon. H. Starnes' expenses to Ottawa........ . $ 20 00
            Hon. H. Starnes and H. T. Machin's expenses
               to New York.................................   210 26
                                           $ 230 26

LOAN OF 1880.

1880.
April 22—Hon. J. Wurtele's expenses to France :
                          First trip. .... $ 800 00
July   9—   Second trip...................   2,300 00
                                           $3,100 00

LOAN OF 1888.

1887.
Sept. 9—Hon. D. A. Ross' expenses to New York... $ 509 14
  "   14—Hon. J. Shehyn's expenses to New York....   546 80
1888.
Jan.   9—Hon. H. Mercier's expenses to France......   2,480 00
Mar. 16—Hon. P. Garneau's expenses to France......   416 71
                                           $3,958 65

RE-CONVERSION OF PUBLIC DEBT.

1889.

Sept. 21—Hon. P. Garneau's expenses to Europe..... $1,961 66
        Hon. J. Shehyn's expenses to Europe...... 1,955 27
        C. J. Burroughs, secretary........ $250 00
        C. J. Burroughs, expenses con-
          nected with trip to Europe.. 275 00
                                    525 00
                                                  4,441 93

LOAN OF 1891.

1891.

Mar. 10—Hon. J. Shehyn, to meet travelling ex-
        penses .... $ 500 00
        B. M. Stocking, tickets to Paris for Pre-
          mier, Treasurer, Secretary and ser-
          vant.. 664 00
        J. Eveleigh & Co., valises, etc................ 54 00
        Hon. J. Shehyn's drafts, April to Sept., for
          Hon. H. Mercier and his own ex-
          penses.............................. ..... 7,584 24
                                                  8,802 24

In addition to this last item there was a commission in connection with the culture of Beet Root, composed of the Hon. Messrs. Mercier, Bernatchez and Ness. This commission was also in Europe at the same time the loan of 1891 was being effected. The expenses of this commission amount to $11,115.85. It will thus be seen that up to the present date the expenses of these gentlemen in Europe last year in connection with the Loan and the Beet Root Sugar Commission cost the country $19,918.09.

COMMISSION RE LUNATIC ASYLUMS AND GAOLS.

Under this heading the Hon. Messrs. Robidoux and Charles Langelier made a so-called trip to the United States to inspect the Lunatic Asylums and Gaols, and in the course of their enquiry they found it necessary to visit the Southern States and the Island of Cuba. They returned after about a month's voyage and their bill against the Province is $5,006.26.

48

CONCLUSION.

The foregoing figures of cash operations and assets and liabilities, and respecting the late administration under Mr. Shehyn's management, and taking, as stated before, his own classification, show that—

1st. The total deficit for four years ending 30th June, 1888, 1889, 1890 and 1891, between ordinary receipts and ordinary payments, was $528,572 70.

2nd. In addition, the so-called "special expenditure," exclusive of railways, aggregated $2,674,243 82, or an average of $668,560 95 per year.

That for Railways aggregated $3,037,960 53, or an average of $759,490 13 per year.

And these special and railway expenditures have had to be paid out of borrowed money.

3rd. In the same four years the so-called ordinary expenses have increased as follows :—

Ordinary expenses as above, 1891.......................................$4,095,520 45
Ordinary expenses in 1886, as per Public Accounts that
    year, page 16... 3,032,771 45
                         Increase 1891 over 1886....................$1,062,749 00

4th. Our nett debt has increased as follows :—

Nett debt 17th December, 1891 ....$24,423,683 62
Nett debt 17th January, 1887.. 11,389,167 11
                  Increase...... ....$13,034,516 51

5th. This is without considering the results of 1891-1892, which will make the situation much worse.

6th. During the whole period Mr. Shehyn had also the advantage of arrears of taxes on commercial corporations and annual revenue from same source, as well as an increase on the ground rents for timber limits, and increase from liquor and other licenses.

These were as follows :—

Arrears Commercial Corporation Tax.............................$558,393 00
Annual collection Commercial Corporation Tax.......about. 130,000 00
Annual increase ground rents on Timber Limits......about. 140,000 00
Annual increase one year from Licenses ....about. 150,000 00

Without these increases what would Mr. Shehyn's position have been ?

In conclusion I can only say I have already spoken at the Drill Shed on the Constitutional question. I accept my share of the responsibility in the dismissal of **Mr.**

Mercier and the appeal to the country. None can complain but the people, and in their hands we leave the whole matter. The Baie des Chaleurs Railway matter and the subsequent disgraceful plunderings of the Public Chest, justify our action, and we ask the people to confirm this.

As to the figures and statements I have given you candidly to-night the figures showing you the result of the Mercier administration for a little over four and a half years.

These shew clearly it has been reckless, extravagant and corrupt beyond measure. It has put in jeopardy the stability of the Province, smurched its credit and threatens its ruin, and it remains for you, the people of the Province, to decide whether it is to continue.

I have thrown the responsibility upon you, and the vote of the electorate on the 8th March next will decide.

I sincerely trust that the true patriotism of the people will rise to the situation and declare that this state of affairs must cease and the plundering of the Provincial Treasury be put a stop to.

Statement of original Estimates of Expenditure, as submitted to the House by the Provincial Treasurer for the years 1887-'88, 1888-'89, 1889-'90 and 1890-'91 respectively, and actual Expenditure for the same periods, as per Public Accounts.

TREASURY DEPARTMENT, QUEBEC, 9th January, 1892.

	1887-'88 Estimates	1887-'88 Expenditure	1888-'89 Estimates	1888-'89 Expenditure	1889-'90 Estimates	1889-'90 Expenditure	1890-'91 Estimates	1890-'91 Expenditure
Public Debt	$1,074,363.67	$1,103,710.94	$1,100,153.00	$1,134,789.51	$1,186,715.50	$1,259,406.88	$1,176,055.32	$1,271,506.33
Legislation	181,785.00	228,994.88	190,850.00	231,812.90	207,142.50	312,948.81	206,323.10	281,078.74
Civil Government	192,850.19	208,677.61	219,776.00	236,987.39	233,917.00	255,144.20	239,742.00	269,660.07
Administration of Justice	471,122.98	554,146.07	495,938.98	559,120.46	476,316.00	599,883.50	515,918.73	679,006.18
Public Instruction	371,085.00	375,459.58	389,645.00	389,835.00	387,185.00	386,485.00	401,860.00	402,106.34
Agriculture	76,150.00	97,700.00	114,100.00	94,061.93	94,350.00	98,636.54	123,450.00	112,737.09
Colonization and Immigration	79,000.00	94,800.00	133,000.00	131,747.00	147,550.00	151,015.53	132,650.00	132,891.80
Public Works and Buildings	58,906.76	145,096.91	97,300.76	116,164.23	95,906.76	148,841.23	94,906.76	139,612.83
Lunatic Asylums	230,000.00	241,000.00	230,000.00	230,000.00	215,000.00	230,000.00	210,000.00	269,143.33
Charities	39,316.00	33,316.00	41,506.00	41,956.00	44,206.00	44,206.00	47,389.33	47,729.33
Miscellaneous Services	226,250.00	234,464.32	265,100.00	328,509.11	259,881.75	348,428.91	277,350.00	436,342.00
Special Expenditure	414,500.00	637,767.76	414,363.12	397,638.40	270,653.93	818,583.51	912,183.00	820,254.15
Railway Subsidies	805,406.40	662,275.30	783,500.00	1,076,647.00	765,000.00	343,417.97	540,000.00	955,620.26
	$4,220,736.00	$4,623,409.37	$4,475,222.86	$4,969,268.93	$4,389,024.44	$4,996,998.08	$4,877,828.24	$5,817,678.45

H. T. MACHIN,

Assistant Provincial Treasurer.